The Maiden of Northland

A Hero Tale of Finland

retold by **Aaron Shepard**   illustrated by **Carol Schwartz**

*For the students of Arnold Elementary
Enjoy the adventure!
Carol Schwartz
1999*

A t h e n e u m   B o o k s   f o r   Y o u n g   R e a d e r s

How to Say the Names

Aila	I-luh
Annikki	ON-nik-kee
Ilmarinen	EEL-muh-RIN-nen
Joukahainen	YO-kuh-HI-nen
Louhi	LO-hee
Vainamoinen	VI-num-MER-nen

Prologue

Not so long ago, in the tiny, isolated villages of Finland, where prolonged summer days give way to endless winter nights, people would pass the time by singing the many adventures of their favorite heroes: the mighty, magical men and women of ancient days.

They sang of old Vainamoinen, greatest of sages and magicians, who helped create the world but never could find a woman to wed him.

They sang of his friend and ally Ilmarinen, first among craftsmen, the blacksmith who forged the dome of the heavens.

They sang of Louhi, the ancient lady of Northland, whose crafty wit and magical powers made her a worthy opponent for Vainamoinen himself.

And they sang of Aila, Louhi's lovely daughter, who captured the hopes of the two old friends and drew them as rivals to the shores of Northland.

The songs endure, the heroes live. . . .

The Battle of Song

I find my power in a chant.
I win my magic from a song.
But can I find a woman's warmth?
And can I win a maiden's love?

This sad song sang Vainamoinen,
old magician, ancient sage,
as his sleigh ran over the marsh,
sped along the lake.
The wind blew his beard,
the summer sun warmed him.

Around the bend
another sleigh raced,
full speed down the trail
the young man pressed.
No time to stop,
no time to turn aside.

The horses swerved,
the sleighs collided.
Shaft wedged against shaft,
harnesses entangled.
The drivers nearly tumbled out.

Astonished, they eyed each other,
waited for words.
The horses dripped sweat,
pawed the ground.

"Young man!" said Vainamoinen.
"Who are you who drives so recklessly?"

"I am Joukahainen," said the youth.
"Old man, who are you who got in my way?"

"I am Vainamoinen," said the sage.
"Now move your sleigh and let me by,
for youth must ever give way to age."

Said Joukahainen,
"That was in a time long past.
Age must now make way for youth,
for the young know more than the old!"

"Is this true?" scoffed Vainamoinen.
"Say what you know, then.
Share this great knowledge!"

Said Joukahainen,
"Yes, I know a thing or two.
I know the fire is on the hearth,
and the smokehole near the ceiling.
A plow in the south is pulled by horse,
and in the north by reindeer.
The pike feeds on salmon
and lays its eggs when frost arrives."

"An infant knows as much!" said Vainamoinen.
"What else can you offer?"

Said Joukahainen,
"Iron comes from ore,
copper from the rock.
Water is born from the mountains,
fire from the heavens.
The titmouse was the first of birds,
the willow the first of trees."

"A toddler has such wisdom!
Can you furnish nothing better?"

Said Joukahainen,
"Back in the beginning,
the seas were dug out,
and the mountains piled high.

The pillars of the sky were erected,
and the rainbow raised.
The sun and moon were set on their paths,
and the stars scattered in the sky."

"Know yourself a fool," said Vainamoinen.
"For I dug out the seas,
and I piled high the mountains.
I stood among the seven heroes
who erected the pillars of the sky
and raised the rainbow.
And when that was done,
we set the sun and moon on their paths
and scattered the stars in the heavens."

Then declared Joukahainen,
"If my knowledge does not impress you,
my sword may do better.
Old man, draw your blade!"

"My sword stays where it is," said Vainamoinen.
"I would not dirty it on you."

Cried Joukahainen,
"You won't fight?
Then I'll use great magic on you!
I'll chant you to a pig,

change you to a swine.
After that, I'll strike you dead,
throw you on a dunghill!"

Then Vainamoinen grew angry.
He began to chant.
The earth shook,
the sky rumbled.
Water splashed from the lake,
the stones cracked.

Vainamoinen chanted
and the sword of Joukahainen
became lightning bolts across the sky.
His crossbow turned to a rainbow over
    the lake,
his arrows to hawks overhead.

Vainamoinen chanted
and the sleigh of Joukahainen
became a log in the water.
His horse turned to a boulder on the shore,
his whip to a reed on the bank.

Vainamoinen chanted
and the coat of Joukahainen
became a cloud in the sky.

His hat turned to a water lily on the lake,
his belt to a snake among the reeds.

Vainamoinen chanted
and Joukahainen sank in the marshy ground,
up to his waist in the swallowing earth.

Cried Joukahainen,
"Reverse your words,
undo your spells!
I will give you a hat full of silver,
a helmet full of gold."

"Keep your wealth," said Vainamoinen.
"My coffers overflow."
He chanted again,
and Joukahainen sank to his chest.

"Reverse your words,
undo your spells!
I will give you fields for plowing,
meadows for pasture."

"Keep your land.
My farm stretches beyond sight."
He chanted again,
and Joukahainen sank to his chin.

"Reverse your words,
undo your spells!
I will tell you of the fairest woman,
the finest maiden."

Vainamoinen stopped his chant.

Said Joukahainen,
"She is lovely Aila,
maiden of Northland,
daughter of age-old Louhi.
She's called a blossom sweet to smell,
a fruit ripe to pluck.
Her fame spreads far,
the suitors gather.
But no proposal has she smiled on,
no suitor given the nod."

Then Vainamoinen chanted again.
He reversed his words,
undid his spells.
Joukahainen rose from the marshy ground,
up from the swallowing earth.

The cloud became again his coat.
The water lily turned back to a hat,
the snake to a belt.

The log became again his sleigh.
The boulder turned back to a horse,
the reed to a whip.

The lightning became again his sword.
The rainbow turned back to a crossbow,
the hawks to arrows.

The young man wept in shame.
The old man raced for home.

The Rivals

Lively Annikki,
hardworking maiden,
sister to the great smith Ilmarinen,
washed laundry on the jetty,
cleaned clothes before dawn.
She dipped the garments in the sea,
laid them on the stone,
beat them with the paddle.
The sun rose,
the waves glistened.

Annikki paused from her work,
looked about her,
welcomed the morning light,
the summer air.
Far south along the shore,
she noticed a speck on the water,
a tiny dot on the sea.

Said Annikki,
"If you are a flock of geese,
rise now into the air.
If you are a school of salmon,
dive beneath the water.
If you are a boat,
sail closer."

It sailed closer, got bigger.
It was a boat painted red,
decorated with gold and silver,
adorned with a red sail.
Vainamoinen held the rudder.

"Vainamoinen!
Where are you headed?"

The old man answered,
"I'm off to fish for salmon."

Said Annikki,
"Since when are salmon caught
without a net,
without a spear?
Tell the truth, Vainamoinen!
Where are you headed?"

"I'm off to hunt for geese."

"Since when are geese hunted
without a crossbow,
without a dog?
Don't lie to me, Vainamoinen!
Where are you headed?"

"I'm off to fight a battle."

"Since when is a battle fought
without a hundred men,
a hundred weapons?
Enough lies, Vainamoinen!
Tell the truth,
or I'll curse you for a liar,
send your boat below the waves!"

"No need of that!
I'll tell you now.

I'm off to court Aila,
maiden of Northland,
daughter of age-old Louhi."

When Annikki heard these words,
she dropped her paddle,
left her washing,
picked up the hem of her long skirt,
ran to her brother's house.

At the anvil stood Ilmarinen,
great smith, eternal artisan,
who formed the dome of the sky
and left not a hammer mark on it.
His skin was black with soot,
his hair thick with ash.
The metal glowed,
the hammer rang.

"Brother! Dawdler! Footdragger!
A year you've taken
to make the horseshoes,
shoe the horse,
fix your sleigh,
paint it red,
decorate it—

all to court Aila,
maiden of Northland.
But not all men take time like you.
A red boat sails to Northland,
and Vainamoinen sails it!"

Ilmarinen gave a cry,
let go his tongs,
threw down his hammer.
"Sister, quick,
prepare the sauna."

She lit the fire,
drew the water,
prepared a whisk,
made the soap.
The smith scrubbed off
the soot of winter,
the ash of spring.
His skin shone,
his hair shimmered.

"Sister, quick,
my finest clothes."

She brought him boots,
a shirt of linen,
woolen jacket,
high-peaked hat.
He put them on
and shone still brighter,
so handsome now
she barely knew him.

His swiftest horse
the smith now harnessed,
hitched it to his sleigh,
the one he'd painted red,
the one he'd decorated.
The shafts held fourteen bells—
seven silver ones
that called like cuckoos,
seven golden ones
that sang like bluebirds.

Off rushed Ilmarinen,
onward raced the smith.
He sped along the sandy beach,
coursed across the shingle.
Sand beat back at him from the hooves,
sea water sprayed him.
The red boat came in sight.

"Vainamoinen!
Where are you headed?"

"I'm off to court Aila,
maiden of Northland,
daughter of age-old Louhi."

Said Ilmarinen,
"Then two suitors will she choose from.
But make a pact with me, old comrade.
No matter what her choice,
no matter who she favors,
let no enmity come between us,
no feud to spoil our friendship."

Said Vainamoinen,
"No enmity shall come between us,
no feud to spoil our friendship."

The boat sliced the water.
The sleigh skimmed the bank.

The Maiden

Age-old Louhi,
dame of Northland,
sat on the floor before her mill,
turning, turning the top stone,
feeding grain through the hole,
slowly grinding the day's flour.
The millstone rumbled,
the woman grumbled.

Lovely Aila,
maiden of Northland,
sat at the loom,
slinging the shuttle,
banging the beater,
weaving cloth for woolen garments.
The shuttle rang,
the maiden sang.

Outside, the watchdog barked.
Said Louhi to her daughter,
"I have grain to grind,
bread to bake.
Look to the dog,
see what bothers it."

"Mother,
I have cloth to weave,
yarn to spin.
I can't spare a moment,
can't stop for an instant."

Muttered Louhi,
"Young women are always busy,
even when they lounge in bed."

She went outside,
walked to the farmyard's edge.
A red boat sped across the bay,
a red sleigh coursed along the shore.

Louhi rushed inside.
"Daughter, good news!
If my eyes don't fail me,
Vainamoinen comes to court,
Ilmarinen comes to wed.
No maid ever chose from two such heroes—
Vainamoinen, rich and wise,
Ilmarinen, skilled and handsome.
Which do you prefer?"

"Mother, why choose either?
Do you wish me gone so soon?
Let me stay here,
to stroll through the wood
and dance in the meadow.
A wife's work starts before dawn,
ends long after dusk.
She has no time to sing to birds,
no chance to pluck the berries."

Said Louhi,
"This is child's talk,
not a woman's.
You can't stay here forever,
can't always be a girl!"

"But can't I be a girl a little longer?
Must every maiden be a wife
before her fifteenth year?"

"It's true you could wait awhile,"
   said Louhi.
"But even if you aren't ready,
we might gain from the ardor of
   these heroes.
I have a plan.
Daughter, quick,
dress in your finest.

Wear ribbons of red,
ornaments of gold and silver."

Not long after,
Vainamoinen landed,
jumped from his boat;
Ilmarinen pulled up,
leaped from his sleigh.
Shoulder to shoulder
they rushed through the gate,
strode over the farmyard,
threw open the cabin door,
pushed their way inside.

Then both stopped amazed.
Lovely Aila stood there,
dressed in her finest,
wearing ribbons of red,
ornaments of gold and silver.
Her cheeks glowed,
her eyes danced.

Said Louhi,
"A greeting to the famous heroes!
A welcome to the two great men!
And what could you seek in Northland?"

"Your daughter in marriage,"
said Vainamoinen.
"The maiden as wife,"
said Ilmarinen.

Said Louhi,
"If only there were two of her,
then she could go with both!
But as things are,
a contest must be held."

"What is the contest?"
asked Vainamoinen.

"You each must make for me a gift,
something never seen before.
I'll decide whose gift is finest,
whose present has greatest value."

"And what is the prize?"
asked Ilmarinen.

"The winner asks the maid to marry,
proposes to my fair daughter."

Warmly smiled the maiden.
Swiftly beat two hearts.

The Sampo

Ilmarinen,
great smith, eternal artisan,
chose a site for his Northland smithy,
selected a piece of stony ground.
He built a forge,
made a bellows,
set up an anvil,
poured charcoal in the forge,
started the fire.
Bare-chested stood the smith,
pumping the bellows,
fanning the embers.
The soot rose,
the ashes fell.

Said Ilmarinen,
"Now I'll make something never seen before—
a sampo for age-old Louhi,
a magic mill for Northland.
I'll make it from the feather of a swan,
the milk of a barren cow,
a single grain of barley,
the fleece of a lamb in summer."

He added them to the fire,
melted them down—

the feather of a swan,
the milk of a barren cow,
a single grain of barley,
the fleece of a lamb in summer.
He gripped the bellows,
pumped one hour,
pumped a second,
then a third.

The smith leaned over,
looked in the forge.
Among the coals
a sword was forming,
a hilt of gold
with a blade of silver.

"Forge me!" said the sword.
"Each day I'll cut a head off,
maybe two!"

Said Ilmarinen,
"The gift I seek serves life,
not death."
He broke up the sword,
stirred it around.

Again he gripped the bellows,
pumped one hour,
pumped a second,
then a third.

The smith leaned over,
looked in the forge.
Among the coals
a crossbow was forming,
a bow of gold
with an arrow of silver.

"Forge me!" said the crossbow.
"Each day I'll pierce two hearts,
and maybe three!"

Said Ilmarinen,
"The gift I seek serves love,
not hate."
He broke up the crossbow,
stirred it around.

Ilmarinen gave up pumping,
instead called out in four directions,
"South wind blow!
West wind gust!

East wind bluster!
North wind blast!"

The south wind blew,
the west wind gusted,
the east wind blustered,
the north wind blasted.
Embers shot from the forge,
ashes danced in the air.

The smith leaned over,
looked in the forge.
Among the coals
a sampo was forming,
a mill of gold
with a top of silver.

"Forge me!" said the sampo.
"Each day I'll grind a bin of flour—
some to bake,
some to sell,
some to save for later.
You'll need no hand to turn my top.
The top will turn itself!"

Said Ilmarinen,
"This is the gift I seek,

the present I hoped for."

He lifted the sampo from the coals,
hammered it on the anvil,
heated it in the forge,
hammered, heated, hammered,
till the sampo was perfect,
till the mill was done.

The smith rejoiced.
The sampo gleamed.

The Kantele

Vainamoinen,
old magician, ancient sage,
took an ax,
took a carving knife,
walked in the Northland woods,
strode through the ancient forest.
Birds chattered,
creatures scattered.

Said Vainamoinen,
"Now I'll make something never seen before—
a kantele for age-old Louhi,
a five-string instrument for Northland."

He found an alder.
He asked, "Is a kantele within you?"

The alder answered,
"My wood is rotten,
my timber infested.
No kantele is within me."

He found a pine.
"Is a kantele within you?"

The pine answered,
"My wood is gnarled,
my timber knotty.
No kantele is within me."

He found a birch.
"Is a kantele within you?"

The birch answered,
"My wood is sound,
my timber clear.
A fine kantele is within me."

Vainamoinen felled the birch,
cut a section from the log.

He carved the body of a kantele,
whittled the frame of the instrument.
Tuning pegs came from an oak branch,
strings from his own long beard.

The kantele was ready.
He took it to the river's edge,
sat himself on a rock,
set the instrument on his lap.
His fingers stroked the strings,
his thumbs caressed them.
The forest grew still,
the river quiet.
Never was such sweet music heard,
such lovely melody given life.

Vainamoinen played
and the forest animals gathered.
Squirrels rested in the branches above,
rabbits and foxes at his feet.
The elk stood at his side,
the bear and the wolf
sat among the rest.

Vainamoinen played
and the river fish assembled.

Pike and salmon swam in close,
carp and perch and whitefish
mingled in the reeds.

Vainamoinen played
and the birds flocked to listen.
The hawk and the eagle perched in the trees,
swans and geese floated on the river.
Buntings, larks, and chaffinches
landed everywhere,
settled on his shoulders.

Vainamoinen played
and all things wanted to hear.
The reeds leaned forward,
the trees bent over.
The river slowed to catch the tune,
the rocks hastened to learn the rhythm.
Even the sun turned an ear,
straining to hear the rising tones.

The old man wept for joy.
The kantele resounded.

The Contest

Age-old Louhi,
dame of Northland,
clasped her hands in eagerness,
held her breath in waiting.
Two suitors were before her,
two heroes bearing gifts.

Said Louhi,
"Tell me, Vainamoinen,
what present have you brought,
what gift for the maiden's mother?"

"Something never seen before—
a kantele,
a five-string instrument."

He set it on his lap,
strummed the strings.
Lovely music filled the room,
sweet melody filled the cabin.
Tears came to Vainamoinen's eyes,
to Ilmarinen's,
to Louhi's.

The mice peeked out,
crept from the walls.

The old man finished,
handed the kantele to Louhi.
She set it on her lap,
picked at the strings.
Harsh twanging filled the room,
sharp discord filled the cabin.
Vainamoinen covered his ears,
so did Ilmarinen.
The mice squealed,
rushed back in the walls.

Louhi tossed the kantele on the table.
"What good the instrument without the player?
And even if I made sweet sounds,
would it get the farmwork finished,
the housework done?"

She turned to the second suitor.
"Tell me, Ilmarinen,
what present have you brought,
what gift for the maiden's mother?"

"Something never seen before—
a sampo,
a magic mill."

He set it above a bin,
poured grain in the hole.
The top turned,
spun faster,
faster.
The sampo filled the bin with flour—
some to bake,
some to sell,
some to save for later.
No hand was needed,
the top turned itself.

Louhi clapped her hands in joy.
"A blessing on you, Ilmarinen!
So much drudgery you've done away with,
so much toil you've ended!
How many hours I've turned and turned
and turned that wretched millstone!
Yours is the finest gift,
the present of greatest value!"

She went to the door,
called to her daughter.

"Come in, fair one!
Hear the smith,
consider his plea."

Lovely Aila ran from the fields,
skipped in from her playing.
Her eyes shone,
her cheeks flushed.

Said Ilmarinen,
"Will you come with me
to be my lifelong partner,
to be my friend forever?"

Aila laughed and said,
"I would never marry a smith!
Better no husband at all
than one who's always black with soot,
forever covered in ash.
No, I will not go with you
to be your lifelong partner,
to be your friend forever!"

Then said Vainamoinen,
"If the smith doesn't suit you,
consider another!

Will you come with me
to be my lifelong partner,
to be my friend forever?"

Aila laughed and said,
"I would never marry a man so old!
Better no husband at all
than one too wise to have fun,
too ancient to play with.
No, I will not go with you
to be your lifelong partner,
to be your friend forever!"

Then out ran lovely Aila,
back to her fields,
back to her playing.
The two men stood astonished
and ashamed.

Said Vainamoinen,
"If the maid won't marry,
the gifts must be returned."

"Not so," said Louhi.
"The winner earned the right to ask.
The answer was not promised."

Said Ilmarinen,
"No present is due to scheming women,
no gift to deceivers of men."

He reached for the sampo.
Then Louhi began to chant.
The air thickened,
the light dimmed.
Louhi chanted
and the mice were drawn from the walls,
grew tall,
became men with swords.
They laid hands on Ilmarinen,
advanced on Vainamoinen.

Vainamoinen snatched the kantele,
started strumming,
started plucking,
played a ditty,
a catchy tune.
The guards were swaying,
their legs were twitching,
their feet were lifting,
their arms were swinging.
They couldn't help it,
they couldn't stop it.
They dropped their swords,

they joined their hands.
They danced,
they twirled,
they jumped,
they spun.

"Stop this dancing!"
screamed the dame of Northland.
Then Louhi was swaying,
her legs were twitching,
her feet were lifting,
her arms were swinging.
She couldn't help it,
she couldn't stop it.
She danced,
she twirled,
she jumped,
she spun.

The dance went on
till legs were failing,
arms were dragging,
heads were slumping.
One by one,
the men fell down,
fell into slumber.
Then at last

old Louhi slid down,
slid into sleep.

Ilmarinen grabbed the sampo,
Vainamoinen clutched the kantele.
They ran to the shore,
boarded the red boat,
launched it,
hoisted the sail.
Vainamoinen took the rudder,
chanted a stiff breeze,
steered to the south.

They sailed an hour,
sailed a second,
then a third.
Then declared Ilmarinen,
"A good trick that was,
a fine escape!
Let's sing a song of victory,
a poem of rejoicing!"

Said Vainamoinen,
"The shore of Northland is still in sight.
Better wait to see your own
before you sing of victory."

But Ilmarinen didn't listen.
He sang a song of victory,
a poem of rejoicing.
But his voice was bad,
his pitch way off.
A crane on a nearby island took fright,
flew off squawking toward the north.
It was squawking when it got to Northland,
squawking still over Louhi's cabin.
The woman woke,
the dame arose.

Cried Louhi,
"They've taken the sampo,
stolen the gift!"

Louhi ran to the shore,
boarded a boat,
launched it,
hoisted the sail.
She took the rudder,
chanted a stiff breeze,
steered to the south.
She sailed one hour,
sailed a second,
then a third.

While Louhi sailed,
Vainamoinen said to the smith,
"Climb the mast,
say what you see."

Ilmarinen climbed the mast,
looked toward Northland.
"A cloud of mist is on the water."

Said Vainamoinen,
"That's no mist."

An hour passed, he said again,
"Climb the mast,
say what you see."

"An island sits above the waves."

Said Vainamoinen,
"That's no island."

An hour passed, he said once more,
"Climb the mast,
say what you see."

"A boat draws near
and Louhi sails it!"

Then Louhi's voice came over the water.
"You phony heroes,
thieves from women!
Return the sampo!
Give back the gift!"

Louhi began to chant.
Dark clouds gathered,
thunder rumbled.
Winds buffeted the red boat,
tore at the red sail.
The waves rose,
broke over the side.

Said Vainamoinen,
"Toss me your tinderbox!"

Ilmarinen tossed it.
Vainamoinen opened the box,
took out the flint,
threw the tiny stone in the sea.
He chanted
and the flint became a reef,
a barrier hidden under the waves.

Louhi's boat reached the reef,
struck the barrier.

The hull split,
the stern burst,
the sides broke to pieces,
the mast came crashing.
Louhi fell in the water,
clung to the wreckage.

Then Louhi chanted again
and she became a giant eagle.
Each wing was longer than a hero,
each talon stronger than a sword.
She rose from the water screeching,
flew after the red boat.

Cried Ilmarinen,
"An eagle comes,
a bird named Louhi!"

The giant eagle bore down,
landed on the masthead,
jumped to the yardarm.
The boat leaned sideways,
nearly keeled over.
The kantele slid,
bounced,
dropped over the side.

Vainamoinen saw it drop,
watched it sink.

Shrieked Louhi,
"The sampo's mine!
I'll take the gift!"
She spread her wings,
got ready to jump.
Cried Vainamoinen,
"Strike at her claws!"

Ilmarinen drew his sword,
struck at her claws.
It left not a mark,
never hurt her.

Then Vainamoinen drew up the rudder,
lifted it over his head,
smashed it down on Louhi's talons.
The claws shattered,
the talons were crushed—
all but one.

Louhi screeched,
half fell, half jumped,
landed in the boat.
She reached with the one claw left,
hooked it under the sampo's top,

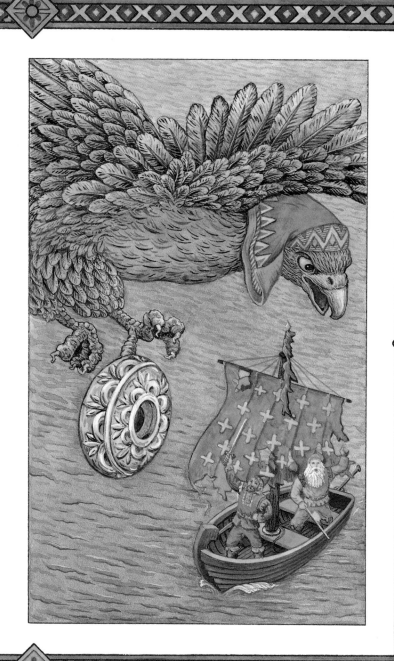

spread her wings,
rose with the sampo into the air.
But her claw gripped the top
and not the bottom.
The bottom slid free,
fell,
plummeted,
down,
down,
hit the waves,
sank in the sea.

Shrieking, screeching,
Louhi flew northward,
bearing home a piece of present,
clutching half of the finest gift.

The sky grew clear.
The sea grew calm.

The Homecoming

Vainamoinen,
old magician, ancient sage,
steered the boat toward shore,

docked it at the jetty.
Ilmarinen,
great smith, eternal artisan,
leaped from the boat,
jumped to the pier.
The red boat rocked,
the sea birds flocked.

Said Ilmarinen,
"Old comrade!
We've lost the two fine gifts,
the things never seen before.
Gone is the kantele,
gone is the sampo.
We come home now with nothing!"

But Vainamoinen wept and sang,

Another kantele can be made.
Another sampo might be forged.
But who can make a woman's warmth?
And who can forge a maiden's love?

About the Story

The Maiden of Northland is based on the *Kalevala* (pronounced KOL-ev-ul-uh), the great national epic of Finland. The *Kalevala* was compiled in the 1800s by Elias Lönnrot—physician, literary scholar, linguist—who was inspired by the nationalist philosophy of his times to uncover a literary heritage for the Finnish people. His medical circuits and research trips took him to outlying villages on both sides of Finland's border with Russia, where he recorded Finnish folk poems, called *runes,* performed by local singers.

These poems, along with many collected by other researchers, were combined by Lönnrot into what is considered the most important book ever to appear in Finland. His epic became a pillar of Finnish nationalism, helping to generate a new pride in national identity, a revival of the Finnish language, and an independence movement that eventually won Finland its freedom from Russian rule.

Today, every Finnish boy and girl knows stories from the *Kalevala* and studies the epic in school. Children, streets, towns, and businesses are named after *Kalevala* characters, and Finnish art, music, dance, and theater frequently draw on *Kalevala* themes. Internationally, the *Kalevala* is recognized as a masterpiece of world literature.

For this retelling, I have drawn on not only the *Kalevala* itself, but also on Lönnrot's two preliminary versions of the epic and on variant runes collected in Lönnrot's time and later. In place of the runes' distinctive trochaic tetrameter I have employed free verse, but I've retained other characteristic elements, such as stock epithets, structural repetition, and parallelism. The maiden's name, Aila, is my own invention.

The following notes may help in understanding particular elements of the story.

Transportation. Finland is a land mostly of forests, lakes, rivers, and marshes, and in the absence of paved roads during *Kalevala* times, wheeled vehicles were impractical. In the winter, when all waterways were frozen and snow covered everything, the sleigh was the only vehicle of transportation. In the summer—the time of this story—both boats and sleighs were used, with the sleighs running over bare ground.

Magic. The descriptions of magic in the *Kalevala* have survived from an ancient time when shamanism was an important part of Finnish tribal life. A similar belief pattern has been found in existing tribal cultures around the world and is thought to have once been common throughout Europe as well.

In the *Kalevala*, magic is made by chanting special runes. These runes often petitioned gods or spirits, or spoke of origins. According to the ancient beliefs, anyone could use the magic runes, but great magicians like Väinämöinen and Louhi knew more runes and more powerful ones than common people did. Another belief was that the spell created by a rune could be undone by singing the words in backward order.

Northland. Lönnrot and many others believed that the old runes looked back to an actual historic conflict between Northland and Kalevala, "the land of Kaleva." (Kaleva was a legendary forebear of the Finns.) But today it is considered much more likely that Northland was a mythological or literary invention rather than a real place.

Sampo (pronounced SOM-po). This originally may have been a shamanistic pillar—a giant good luck charm—but over the centuries, the original meaning of the term was lost. Various singers have described it as a chest, a boat, an eagle, or a mill—but almost always as something magical that bestows prosperity.

Kantele (pronounced KON-tel-eh). This is a type of psaltery often used to accompany rune singing. In its traditional form, the kantele was a five-string instrument small enough to sit on the player's lap. The body was made of a single block of wood such as curly birch, or sometimes alder or pine. Tradition says the strings were first made of horse or human hair, though today they are made of metal. Modern versions of the instrument are about a meter long and have up to thirty-six strings.

References for this retelling included English translations of Lönnrot's *Kalevala* by W. F. Kirby (New York: Dutton, and London: Dent, 1907), Francis P. Magoun, Jr. (Cambridge: Harvard University, 1963), Eino Friberg (Helsinki: Otava Publishing Company, 1988), and Keith Bosley (Oxford and New York: Oxford University, 1989); *The Old Kalevala and Certain Antecedents*, by Elias Lönnrot, translated by Francis P. Magoun, Jr. (Cambridge: Harvard University, 1969); and *Finnish Folk Poetry—Epic*, edited and translated by Matti Kuusi, Keith Bosley, and Michael Branch (Helsinki: Finnish Literature Society, 1977).

For further reading in the *Kalevala* itself, I recommend Friberg's translation, cited above. Good prose retellings for young people include *The Magic Storysinger* by M. E. A. McNeil (Owings Mills, Maryland: Stemmer House, 1993), *Heroes of the Kalevala* by Babette Deutsch (New York: Julian Messner, 1940), and *Land of Heroes* by Ursula Synge (New York: Atheneum, 1978).

Aaron Shepard

For the one I seek—tempting, teasing, entrancing, eluding, drawing me ever to Northland
—A. S.
For Bob, who has given me much love and many adventures
—C. S.

Atheneum Books for Young Readers
An imprint of Simon & Schuster Children's Publishing Division
1230 Avenue of the Americas New York, New York 10020
Text copyright © 1996 by Aaron Shepard   Illustrations copyright © 1996 by Carol Schwartz
All rights reserved including the right of reproduction in whole or in part in any form.
Designed by Becky Terhune
The text of this book is set in Goudy Old Style. The illustrations are rendered in gouache.
Printed in Hong Kong by South China Printing Company (1988) Ltd.
First edition
10 9 8 7 6 5 4 3 2 1

ISBN 0-689-80485-7
Library of Congress Catalog Card Number 95-78300